Yusuf,
Let your imagination
lead you into
Amazing Places!
Edward S. Denecke
2014

What Happens at School When You're Not There?

ISBN: 978-1-9399301-4-9
Library of Congress Control Number: 2013954285

Published by
BELLE ISLE BOOKS
www.belleislebooks.com

an imprint of Brandylane Publishers

What Happens at School When You're Not There?

WRITTEN AND ILLUSTRATED BY

EDWARD J. DENECKE

BELLE ISLE BOOKS
www.belleislebooks.com

What Happens at School
When You're Not There?

is lovingly dedicated:

To my wife, Marilyn, my daughter Rachelle,
my daughter Rebecca, and her husband, Aaron.
Without their help, this story would have remained as lifeless
as a dark and deserted school building.

And to my grandsons, Hudson and Oliver,
in the hopes that one day, they too will discover
how an imagination can turn empty spaces
into amazing places.

What happens at school
when you are not there?
That secret is one
I'm eager to share!

For what I say next
will help you prepare
to spot hidden clues
of goings-on there.

Do you want to know
what janitors see
when children are gone?
Then listen to me.

I'll tell you right now
what happens past three
when teachers go home
and students run free!

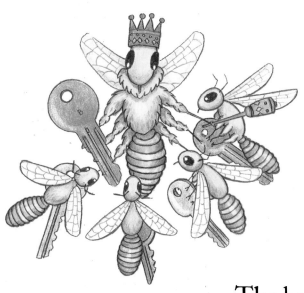

The bees leave their hives
way up in the trees
and spiral to school
upon the night breeze.

They buzz through the air
with janitor keys,
so they can unlock
whatever they please!

Then swarms of these bees
crisscross and careen
throughout the school halls
to follow their queen.

And when she unbolts
each window and screen,
more bees fly inside
than you've ever seen!

Then ants all advance
through heating vent grates
and march underneath
the closed hallway gates.

They strap on ant hats
and slip on ant skates
and pass out ant tools
unpacked from ant crates.

They fly off to work
on paper airplanes
and parachute down
to crumb-filled terrains.

They study their task
with clever ant brains,
then hoist up their food
with paper clip cranes!

The goldfish all leap
incredible heights
to ledges above
their countertop sites.

They hang glide from there
on giant fish kites
to lunchrooms prepared
for fast fish-food fights!

They land with a splash,
and then they all race
to fling those fish flakes
all over the place!

Once that game is done,
the fish will embrace,
then paint silly beards
on each other's face!

Then birds take to flight
from nests on a limb
and swoop into school
on simply a whim.

They fill bathroom sinks
right up to the brim
and stay till they teach
their hatchlings to swim!

They all like to primp
and preen with great care.
Their plumage, they *think*,
is nicely combed hair!

Plucked feathers will fall
and land everywhere,
when birds take their leave
and fly through the air.

Then monkeys all crash
through high ceiling tiles
and land tangled up
in big monkey piles.

They chatter and screech
in rowdy speech styles
and race to the gym
with Cheshire Cat smiles!

These monkeys perform
superb jumping jacks
(with no safety nets)
in high-wire acts!

They swing on long ropes
and eat popcorn snacks,
while baby chimp clowns
hitch rides on their backs!

Wild elephant herds
of Jungle Book tales
from lockers emerge
and leave peanut trails.

With ivory tusks,
they carry milk pails,
while lunch boxes hang
from swishy gray tails!

These great wrinkled beasts
get something to eat
by smashing nuts flat
with their massive feet!

They climb on kids' desks
to dine on this treat.
They push off the books
and squeeze in each seat!

Then gators appear
(not making a sound)
and move like green smoke
across the playground.

They nudge open doors
and look all around
in search of a place
where water is found.

Then they pull a prank
that's really quite cruel:
they flood halls and hold
a slip-and-slide duel!

These gators spread out
and treat the whole school
like it has become
their own swimming pool!

The snakes slither out
quite late in the night
from under the rugs,
when no one's in sight.

When each office space
is dark and closed tight,
they squirm their way in
and switch on each light.

These desk-climbing snakes
then type word for word
the best snake events
that ever occurred!

The snakes love to type
in ways most absurd:
their tongues hit two keys;
their tails hit a third!

When morning is near,
bees relock each lock;
ants hike to ant homes
in fields down the block;

fish leap back in tanks
(each racing the clock!);
and birds hurry out
to rejoin their flock.

The monkeys shut down
their fun circus show,
and elephants all
to lockers tiptoe.

The gators move *fast*.
The snakes travel s l o w.
But they all return
where secrets must go.

Then janitors bring
pine-scented perfumes,
their big garbage cans,
wet mops, and straw brooms.

They sweep, mop, and spray
and use feather plumes
to dust proof away
from hallways and rooms.

They bag evidence
and take it outside.
In dumpsters they toss
the clues that they hide.

And that's why no child
has ever once spied
"what happens" without
their janitor guide!

So now that you've heard
these things I have said,
it's time to do more
than just scratch your head!

The truth won't be found
stashed under your bed.
So search for a hint
in schoolrooms instead!

Your janitors might
know some secrets, too.
If they work at night,
they probably do!

So ask them for help
to find your first clue.
"What Happens at School?"
It's time that you knew!

Acknowledgements

I want to thank the staff of School District 103 in Lincolnshire, Illinois. Their support and encouragement have been a tremendous part of this book ever becoming a reality. The principals, staff, teachers, and especially the students of Laura B. Sprague School in that district inspired all of "the goings-on there" portrayed in these pages.

I want to remember to thank Dr. Sharon M. Carr, who was the first teacher to invite me to read my book to her class, and all the other teachers who have done so since then. I also want to thank Mrs. Mary Lighthall, who based a school musical on an early rendition of this book.

I especially want to thank my niece, Taylor Denecke, who helped me to get my book ready to submit to Belle Isle Books.

I would like to acknowledge the important part that Chris Buczinsky played in helping me learn how to improve the poetry in this book.

Space will not allow me to thank by name all of the other wonderful family and friends who have helped me along the way, but they are appreciated more than words can convey!

About the Author

Edward J. Denecke was born in the Chicago area in 1953, the fourth of twelve children. He loved his big family and devoted parents.

In 1977, he moved to Minneapolis to attend a bible college. There he met and married his wife, Marilyn. After graduating in 1981, they moved back to Illinois, where he spent seven years as a pastor. During those years, he and Marilyn had two daughters, Rebecca and Rachelle.

In 1988, Edward and Marilyn decided they needed a change. And it became a big one. Ed took off his suit and tie and put on a janitor's uniform. Though the transition was hard at first, he soon found his next calling. He *wanted* to be Mr. Ed, the school's custodian!

And in 1994, when he took a day position working in the midst of the students, he discovered how much he enjoyed inventing stories to tell the children. He began describing everyday activities in creative and imaginative ways. Oil mops became alligators. Elephants lived in the boiler room. And ants climbed in through the floor cracks each night to attend night school!

So when a mom asked him to write a children's book about what happened at school when the kids went home, his imagination took flight like a swarm of bees! She was asking Mr. Ed to write a book describing how he cleaned and maintained the building, but instead, the stories he had been telling the children for many years became the spark for this book.

He started to write. And draw. Over the next eighteen years, his story went through many revisions. Teachers began asking him to read his story to their classes. And in 1998, the music teacher at the school where he worked even used the story as the basis for a musical!

Now he's delighted to finally publish his story and share the secret with you. What happens at school when you're not there? It's time that you knew!